This book belongs to ___Jasmine___

Dedicated to...

All the mummies and daddies who are doing a great job even though it might not feel like it

The doctors and nurses and healthcare workers who work so tirelessly to keep us safe and well

My friends and family who I've missed so much and can't wait to see and hug again soon

Auntie Big Mum who was always on hand to listen to my stories as a youngster

A CIP catalogue record for this title is available from the British Library.

Cover and Book Design by: White Magic Studios (www.whitemagicstudios.co.uk)

ISBN 978-1-914366-12-3 (Paperback)
ISBN 978-1-914366-19-2 (Hardback)

First Published (2021)
Maple Publishers
1 Brunel Way
Slough
SL1 1FQ

Rupert and The Silly Bugs

Story by Rupert Glenholme
Illustrated by Gurvinder and Anthony Glenholme

In aid of
Believe in children
Barnardo's

...We had to wash our hands
whilst singing 'Happy Birthday'.
What an odd thing to say.

I was scared and had nasty dreams but we had to stick to the rules.

We couldn't see Nani, Baba,
Grandpa or my cousin Rishaan.

But staying at home made me happy because I could play with Mummy and Daddy and my baby Sister all day.

The doctors and nurses are doing a great job looking after all the poorly people.

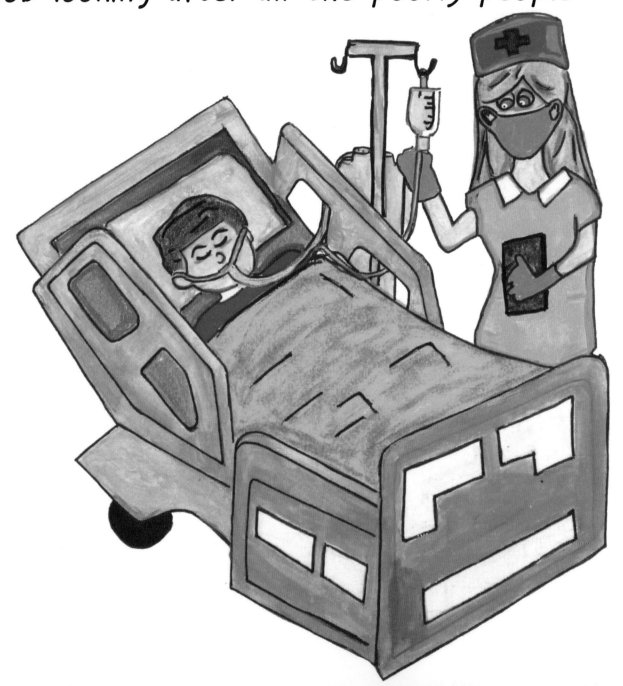

And now the jabs are here they are saving more and more people each day.

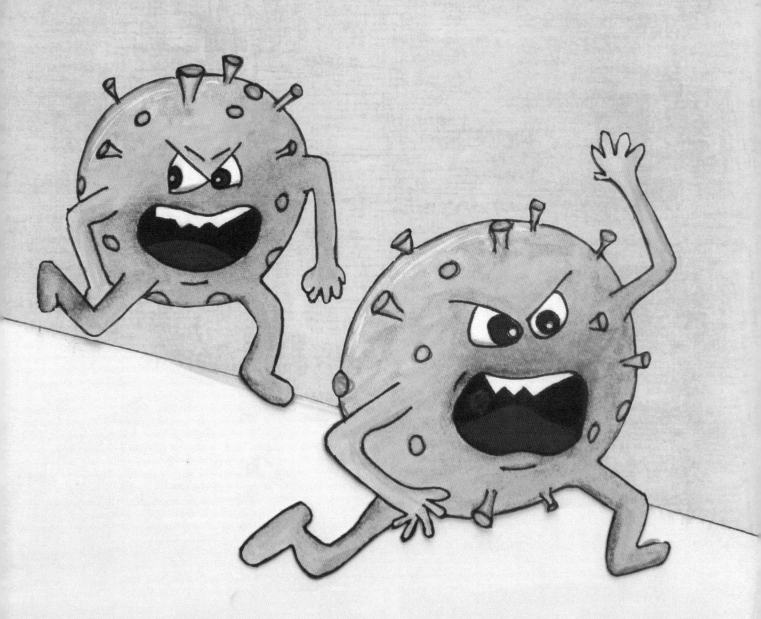

Printed in Great Britain
by Amazon